Downfall of a Droid

'Friends are hard to find, difficult
to leave, impossible to forget.'

Surrounded by a ring of asteroids, the planet of Bothawui is protected by three Jedi Cruisers. In the hangar bay of the command ship the *Resolute*, Anakin Skywalker and R2-D2 are preparing their Delta fighter for combat when they receive an urgent transmission from Obi-Wan Kenobi.

"The Separatist fleet, commanded by General Grievous, is headed your way," says Obi-Wan. "You're heavily outnumbered, Anakin. I advise you to retreat."

"If we run, the Separatists will take control of this sector. I can't let them do that," replies Anakin firmly.

On the other side of the asteroid ring, Grievous's six frigates jump into view from hyperspace and he orders his fleet to fly through the asteroids to engage the Jedi Cruisers.

"All power to the forward shields!" commands Grievous.
"What if they attack us from behind?" questions his captain.
"They can't. The asteroids will protect us," laughs Grievous.

Seeing Grievous's plan, Ahsoka waits impatiently on the bridge of the *Resolute* for his ships to come into firing range.

At the same time, Anakin and a fleet of V-19 fighters are launched, ready to do battle!

l frigates
asteroid
straight for

ire on the
ic Cruiser,"
us.

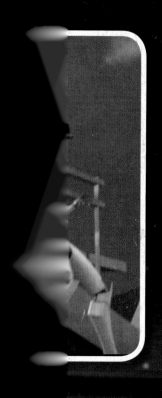

On Anakin's orders the clone fighters retreat – though he continues towards the enemy ships!

"Let's finish them off!" shouts Grievous triumphantly, but he's about to get a shock. "Ahsoka!" calls Anakin. "They're in position! Unveil our little surprise!"

Emerging from their hiding places on the asteroids, AT-TE Walkers open fire on the Separatist Frigates! Captain Rex coordinates the attack, relaying his orders to his soldiers. "All units, fire at will!"

With the Jedi Cruisers firing from the front and the AT-TEs from behind, Grievous is surrounded!
"Get us out of here!" he says, as he watches his ships buckle under the attack.

Realizing the hopelessness of the situation, Grievous jumps into a starfighter and abandons his command ship. He is soon spotted by Anakin, however, who pursues him.

"More speed, Artoo!" calls Anakin, when suddenly – KABOOM! – Grievous's command ship is hit and the whirling debris smashes into Anakin's fighter. R2 is thrown from the starfighter as it bursts into flames!

Anakin wakes up in his bed, still groggy, with Ahsoka and Rex by his side. Uncertain of what happened, he asks for updates.

"Grievous is AWOL, but his fleet of tinnies is nothing but spare parts," Ahsoka tells him proudly. The bad news is that R2-D2 is still missing . . .

Later, Anakin reports to Obi-Wan.

"Congratulations, Anakin. Your resourcefulness always amazes me," Obi-Wan says. But when he hears that R2-D2 is missing, fully programmed with details of tactics and base locations, he is less pleased.

"Find that droid, Anakin. Our necks might very well depend on it."

On board the *Twilight*, Ahsoka introduces Anakin to his replacement astromech droid, R3-S6. "He's gold!" she says excitedly. "A gold droid for a Gold Leader? Of Gold Squadron!"

But Anakin isn't happy: R2-D2 is more than a droid, he's a friend. From the corner, R3 lets out a sad beep as the ship launches into space.

The *Twilight* flies carefully through the battle debris before sighting Anakin's damaged fighter.

"Artoo's gone! He must've escaped," says Anakin happily. But Ahsoka's scanners aren't picking up the missing droid, only the *Vulture's Claw*, a Trandoshan scavenger ship looking for salvage.

Thinking that R2-D2 may have mistakenly been collected as scrap, a disguised Anakin and Ahsoka, with R3 trundling behind, board the *Vulture's Claw*.

They quickly meet its foul-smelling owner, Gha Nachkt. "We're looking for an Artoo unit," says Anakin. "You happen to pick up any recently?"

"No, not for a long time," Gha Nachkt assures them. He guides them down to his cargo hold, leaving them to rummage around his collection. Anakin and Ahsoka can't find any R2 units, but something finds them – deadly IG-86 assassin droids!

Instead of helping, R3 keeps making everything worse! But after a terrifying fight, Anakin and Ahsoka finally overpower the assassin droids, just as Gha Nachkt returns.

"I told you there were no Artoo droids down here! Look at the mess you made!" he says angrily. Realizing Gha Nachkt is right, the Jedi and R3 return to their ship.

As the *Twilight* disengages to return to the Resolute, Gha Nachkt sends a communication . . . to none other than General Grievous!

"I'm en route to the rendezvous point, General. I've got the merchandise you were looking for." Behind him a hidden panel slides open – it's R2-D2!

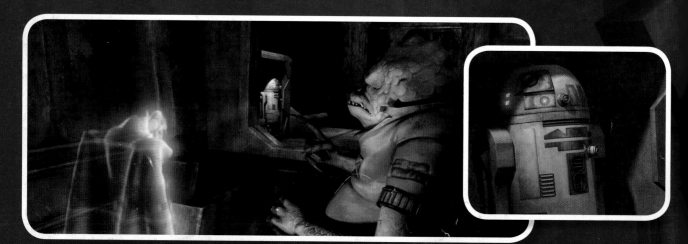

In the war room of the *Resolute*, Anakin reports their failure to find R2. "We have to assume that Artoo was destroyed in the explosion that claimed your ship," says Obi-Wan.

Meanwhile, there has been intelligence that Grievous has a listening post intercepting Jedi transmissions.
"Anakin! Find that base and destroy it," orders Obi-Wan.

Anakin gives Rex and Ahsoka their orders. "I'll sweep the outer corridor, while the rest of your ships focus on the centre."

"Master, you'll need a droid to help you navigate," says Ahsoka, nodding towards R3. Anakin lets out a sigh and, against his better judgement, agrees to let R3 accompany him.

As Gha Nachkt dozes on the bridge, R2-D2 makes his escape . . .

and bumps straight into a patrolling assassin droid! With some quick thinking and even quicker manoeuvring, R2 manages to jettison the droid from the *Vulture's Claw*.

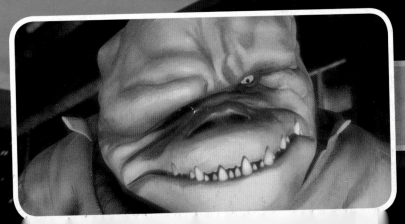

Only to have Gha Nachkt capture him again!

As Anakin brings his starfighter out of hyperspace, he orders R3 to activate the scanners to sweep the area. But R3 switches on the tracking beacon!

"That's Master Skywalker's tracking beacon!" says Ahsoka with alarm, as she hastily organizes reinforcements to investigate.

"Let's hope Grievous didn't hear that. . ." breathes Anakin. But as he deactivates the tracking alarm, two of Grievous's frigates zoom in from hyperspace!

"Yeah, he heard it," sighs Anakin. Apparently in a panic, R3 accidentally ditches the hyperspace ring, leaving them stranded!

As Grievous launches maximum fire-power, Anakin does some fancy flying to escape the deadly missiles.

With R3 beeping fearfully and the laser guns damaged, all looks lost – when the *Twilight* drops out of hyperspace! "Did someone call for help?" asks Ahsoka cheekily.

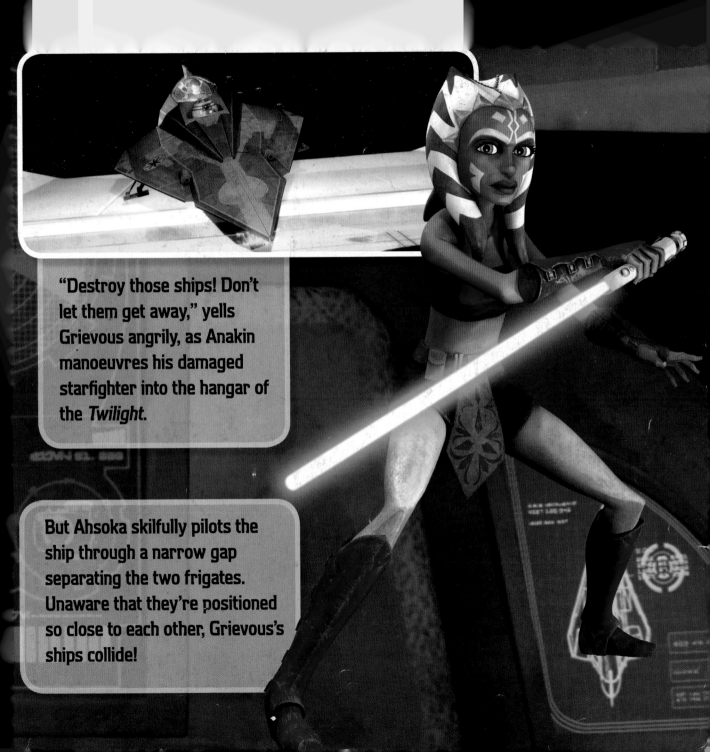

"Destroy those ships! Don't let them get away," yells Grievous angrily, as Anakin manoeuvres his damaged starfighter into the hangar of the *Twilight*.

But Ahsoka skilfully pilots the ship through a narrow gap separating the two frigates. Unaware that they're positioned so close to each other, Grievous's ships collide!

Clear of the frigates, the *Twilight* jumps into hyperspace, leaving Grievous, in his damaged ship, to glare furiously after them.

On their way back to base and safety, Anakin makes a promise to himself.

"Artoo's still out there. I know it. And I'm gonna find him . . . ."